Let Me Get My Glasses:

A Collection of
Short Stories and Poetry

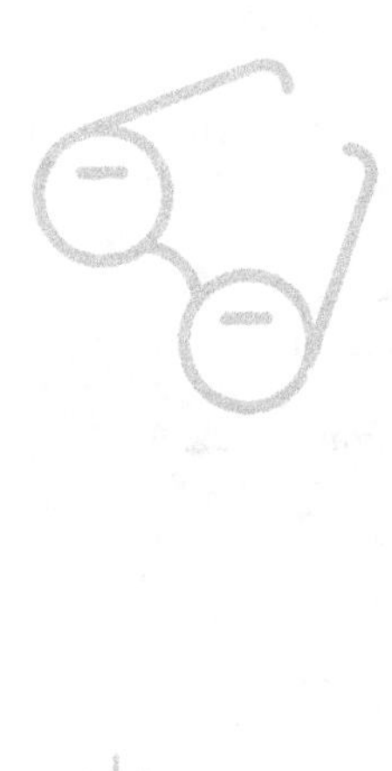

JULIE ANN FAIRLEY

My sisters and I have grown up listening to and reciting my mother's poetry. We were always mesmerized and captured by the power and honesty of her words. The emotion that her words conjured through truth and imagination used to have us laughing and feeling like we were there, and you will too.

Lashon Hollington, Daughter

Julie Ann Fairley is a writer in her own right. She can create magic all by herself. Her ability to make you visualize a picture through her words is simply amazing. JULIE IS A BOSS WRITER ALL BY HERSELF!!!

Valerie Dash, MS Ed.

All those years of jotting down words from dreams, sayings and songs on anything you could get your hands on– brown paper bags, paper towels, matchbook covers, and of course the YELLOW LEGAL PAD– has all come together with celebration. Poetry is a great deal of joy, pain, Hmmmms and Wooooos. Julie Ann has all the above emotions in her poetry and delivers it tastefully. She is full of words, songs, and THUNDER! Loving you so much, Gurl!!!

Your sister from another mother
Denise Campbell

Julie Ann Fairley's storytelling draws you in
immediately. Her writing is raw, real and beautiful.
Julie's words are enthralling, compelling, and engaging.
They make me laugh, cry, and think. She keeps it real.
Thank you for sharing your gift with us!

Denine Chandler-Price,
Avid Reader, Fan and Friend

Julie's book draws you in, makes you laugh, brings
you joy, makes you nostalgic, allows you to believe in
love, then ties it up in a neat little bow of making you
feel like you have been on a cinematic journey but by
a wordsmith. You will not be disappointed by taking a
chance on this amazing read.

TolasTableau.com (blog)

*"No matter what the matter
is, the matter is life."*

-J. California Cooper

Mommy, although you are no longer here, you were
unable to see the full extent of what my writing would
become. However, you knew your only girl had
something… "You write just like my father did." I still
hear your voice telling me that as I sat on the side of
your bed. Auntie, my beautiful Bloneva Applewhite-
Griffin, saw me perform once during her last days. She
simply said, "Ju, you did good. Real good." This book
is dedicated to those who have come before, those who
are with us now and to the future.

Do your best! Bring forth your goodness and your
gifts. Show love and compassion.

Acknowledgements

Thank you, Julia Shaw and Toni Coleman Brown, for giving me guidance throughout this entire process, for encouraging me and orchestrating everything to bring this into fruition.

I thank everyone who has been there for me

Regina Bruce... You are the "crème de la crème" of the English Language. Thank you for the opportunity to sit in your classroom and enjoy being a pupil once again.

Hey Readers,

I have finally done it. I have finally got this work done after all this time. Some of this was written long ago, and as life would have it, many other things have occurred. Some of which we are unable to control, some of which various priority lists ruled. Much to my dismay that age old "procrastinator" emerged. However, at some point, we make up our minds and control our impulses to do other things. Very often the "other things" feel good albeit temporary. Repeatedly, the truth that lies within will surface and summon; the soul will not allow a peaceful rest.

This work is a necessary part of who I am, who I always have been, and who I am unable to deny. Nor will I take that which I am blessed with for granted any longer. It has been said, "If you bring forth what is in you, what is in you will save you. If you do not, it will destroy you!" I have come to know this is so. In my case, I never really felt whole.

Prior to this writing, I had been haunted by the fact that I can express myself using language in a special way. I had been haunted by the fact that the ancestors wanted so much for us. Not only that, but I also sit at my desk each day, staring into a picture of the face of my Floridian grandfather, Caiaphas Applewhite, born in 1895 who authored books – small books. They were 4x6 and 3x5 in the 1940s and 1950s.

A man who worked at the Everglades Club somehow pulled together his resources to create and share his perspectives about life on paper. How could I dare not step up my game? I surely had more of a financial edge than he. I surely inherited a world that offered more opportunities for growth than he. These truths haunted me and summoned me to task, to do better and to grow.

I hope you enjoy Let Me Get My Glasses, a look into the heart of a life journey. Life, and all the uncertainties, has brought me to this place, a place of continuous growth and development. I am about love, peace, joy, and goodness! Truly, that is how I roll.

So, Readers… Take care of yourselves and make sure to "get your glasses," so you can see when you need them throughout the day.

Peace and Blessings,

Julie Ann Fairley

Table of contents

Life As It Was and Our Response to Our Mothers

We lived through some tough times when we were little girls, and our grandparents helped us as best they could. Our mothers did as best they could. The most profound thing we understood was that "there was no better, and that the better came with us!" From a conversation with my loving cousin, Ujimma Masani.

MISCELLANEOUS POEMS

Some Kind of Story

I've been

talkin' for a long time

Talkin' 'bout

this or that

Words

out of my orifice

Transmitted

through air into someone's

ears, head

Ooh! If I could have captured it all on paper

How Many????

Just how many words would I have spoken,
  did I speak,

Say

in a lifetime?

How much was

significant?

shameful?

insignificant?

foolish?

crazy?

funny?

boring?

ridiculous?

Someone else's words?

mean?

sad?
weak?
Weak like a mother hubba
If everything I ever said was on paper
Ooh!
That would be some kind of story

Sometimes

Sometimes
I am alone
and cannot sleep
'cause I am lonely
missing what I used to have
'cause sometimes
it used to be good
Sometimes
I am alone
and I start to cry
'cause I don't like
thinkin' 'bout
what I used to have
or what I used to do
I don't feel good
'cause I am yearnin' for something
that I cannot have
Cannot be where I wanna be
Traveling
back down memory lane
is easy
though painful
useful
'cause that is all there is
and I need to hold on to
something, sometimes
But sometimes ain't doing me
no good

I Do Know

I won't do longing and I
won't do waiting and I
won't do wondering and I
won't do hoping
I won't do crying and I
won't do wishing and I
won't do sorry
I won't do needing
Here… Right now
I won't do yearning
I won't do turning
I won't do sleepless nights
with heartache
warm tears running down my face
I won't do wanting you
here with me right now
in this perfect place
which could be anywhere
where
we are just kickin' it
on any given day
at any moment
I won't do appropriate
times or things always at your convenience or
straight to voicemail
'cause you won't be with me in any form

all those important times you won't be
with me
I am someplace
surrounded by people
feeling so empty and alone
I know
what truth is
you won't be my truth
I love you
and you love me
Oh!
I forgot about the parameters
control
next thing I knew
I was caught up in a situation
satisfying adult needs perhaps
though I do know
I won't do this anymore
This longing, waiting, wondering
hoping, crying, wishing, missing,
sorry, yearning, sleepless nights
shit anymore
I won't do this.
I won't do this!

All Over Again

As I stand in the hot shower
water damn near
burnin' my skin
My eyes fill with tears
mixing with water
won't take away the pain
But if I had one wish right now
I would wish
I could do things all over again
This time
This time
Things would be right
And my tears would be tears of joy
Not pain
My tears would shine as they ran down my cheeks
Reflecting all that is beautiful
This time
This time things would be right.
As I stand in the hot shower
My eyes are closed
And a river runs, flows freely
I am looking at things I care not to remember
I am thinking about things that I wish I didn't know
won't take away the pain
There is so much I can blame
And yet

I choose

At this very moment

To make peace with a past that has followed me
  everywhere

You can run

But you can't hide from the truth

And if I had

Just one wish right now

I'd wish I could do things

All over again.

In The Grip

I see fire
I see rain
while washing dishes in
soap suds
Dawn Be My Awakening!
As winter breezes blow briskly
through my window
feelings emerge
bringing tears to my eyes
'cause I remember!
Music plays
Grandma's face comes to mind
And my father
who was always near
though always farther
than I expected
Can't Believe We're Related…
Clothes spinning, rattling in the machine
children running and playing
in the room
While washing dishes
music plays
I see Grandaddy's face
He didn't know me
but I saw him one time
He just saw my picture

Mommy used to send him pictures
the ones when we were in school
Someday We'd Be Together…
Radiator rattling
my little girl crying
Mommy is always near
even for foolishness
though oblivious to it all
While washing dishes in soap suds
I see friends on missions
that were always possible
during dark nights and frigid days
they ran and ran
till they ran out of money
Someone's knockin' on my door
"Hey Girl,
Let's Get Down on Something"
and away goes trouble down the
                        Drain
Suddenly
his face appears
we were lost in an illusion
Forever and a day
was yesterday
Our children are playing
laughing and calling me

Here with me!
While washing dishes in soap suds
raindrops are falling
and teardrops are crawling
down my face
I took a train ride
a friend gave me some money
to buy food
'cause we ran and ran
till we ran out of money
on missions that were always
possible
during dark nights and frigid days
The children were alone…
I took the train ride
cried all the way home
huddled in a corner
on the D train
there was snot all over my face
A lady handed me a tissue
"What's the matter, Baby?" she said.
My son died last week
He was three years old
There's nobody home
Except my other kids
And I ain't got no food

But I got some money my friend gave me
Everybody says I'm so strong
They just don't know
Guess I'll be all right…
I dried the dishes
and put them away
I will ALWAYS remember.

So Motherfucka, What?

This is me!
Me who is here
Every day by herself
Me who is here
Every night by herself
Me with no lovin'
Other than the love that I got for myself
Sometimes
It's bland!!!!
I can't caress myself
Nor feel my body the way I need
to be felt, rubbed, or kissed
or nuzzled against
So Motherf***er, What?
What can you say to me?
What can you tell me?
I ain't playin' no games with you
'cause this shit ain't funny
This was never in my dreams
Yet
This is the way it is!
So, when the sun rises sometimes
and I open my eyes
I feel things
am aroused by possibilities I envision
And I see you

feel you, smell you, taste you
want you to be near
So, Mother------, What?
Right about now I'm
Annoyed that I had to even
write all this shit
Get my drink on
Play some music
Think about batteries
For that thick piece of
rubber in my closet
to get my shit off
'cause you're someplace else
'cause that's what you need to be doing
And guess what?
I understand
Yeah, I understand
Ain't mad
That's the way it is
And this is me
Full of possibilities
and desire and longing and want
Yet I stay chill
'Cause you're
going through things and gotta do things and
I understand

Yeah, I understand
'cause I've traveled similar roads and then some
But right about now
I'm in a place
that I'd rather not be
And the faces on the television
screen are staring at me
And warm thoughts about you are
crossing my mind
And all I can count are the days gon' by
I close my eyes and wonder
Why
I see you, feel you, smell you, and taste you and
wanna be near
To a man who can stand all this
Chill in the air
With me over here and him over there
I'm in a place
that I'd rather not be
But what can I say
this really is me
Don't know what to do now or what to say
Except
I said what I said, and it is this way
So Motherf***er, What?

He Is Necessary

The following poem, "He Is Necessary" had to be part of this book. It was written years ago by "Tammy" (Tamara Graham). I asked her would she mind if I included it in this work and she replied, "Girl, I forgot all about that poem!" It is an extremely powerful poem.

He is necessary
Like breath to breathing
and loss to grieving
He is necessary
Like seeds to soil
and water to light to
Flourishing
He's nourishing
He's necessary
Like sun block
To white folks and slow inhales to those who smoke
He got my nose so open
That I can smell Mr. Yamaguchi's
Cherry blossoms on some avenue
In Japan…right now
Breathe in, breathe out
He's necessary like
Blood to vital organs

J.P. is to Captain Morgan
And John Henry is to legend
I'm on the edge of some other shit for real.
I need a firm hand
And a strong ass back
I need a conscious mind
With a subtle knack for breathing on the back of my
  neck
I need a prayer monger
Who only wields his authority
In the quiet of my cradle lit bedroom
An intelligent man
Who knows the difference between
Who and whom
I need a tower
So that I may seek refuge
A guard to ward off the pests who seek to sadden me
I need a comedian
Who never stays mad at me
A Diaspora member
Who can remember
Ancient lovemaking secrets
From the walls of long forgotten Mystery Schools.
A handyman who can
Fix everything… my car, the dishes, bills and me
All with just one tool

Unfortunately, I have yet to find him
The chiropractor who can
Work me into proper alignment
He is necessary
Like breasts to infant lips
And Blackstar is to instant hits
He is necessary
Like Vaseline to chapped lips
Travelers checks to long trips
He is necessary
Like pulling me by the hand
The way the moon pulls the tide, and the tide
    pulls the sand
He's necessary like
Pitch black is to night
Like black power is to right
And blue green is to the sea
FOR REAL.
I need a warrior
A true revolutionary
Who can see the future
Whenever he stares at me
I need a ruler in search of a kingdom
Someone who knows
That what rests in me
Is the key to his freedom.

I need a prophet who got me exposed
So, he can see my mind's eye
And what color I like to paint my toes
A fearless man
One who never says maybe
Just that he can
And knows exactly when
To call me baby
A mountain mover with the muscle to prove it
I need him
He is necessary.

Music playin'
Chicken fryin' and
I feel good.
Chicken fryin'
Candles burning
Melodies in the air
I'm thinkin' of him.
But I don't let those
Thoughts
Overwhelm me
Ain't gon' lie though
I WISH HE WERE HERE.

Music playin'
Melodies seem to be
where I need to be
Sayin' stuff
Express yourself
Expressin' myself through
song
Damn!
Chills up and down my arms
I BELIEVE IN DREAMS.

I've been havin'
these parties lately

Sippin' on some of this
and
Some of that
depending on
what I feel
Tonight, it's Harvey's
with a twist of
him holdin' me
or
Grand Marnier
with a twang of
Why did he fuck with me in the first place?
But
IT'S ALL COOL.
Life
In the many splendid ways
You know what they say.
Never too much
Right, Luther?
What am I going to do with
ALL THAT I'M FEELING?

Chicken fryin'
Luther playin'
What does happiness really mean?
I want to do some

shit out of the ordinary
But
I don't want to go to
voicemail
So, I
Leave that alone
Another drink?
Not
DON'T WANNA SWAY...

I sit
the scented candle lights the room
It flickers
I am enveloped in
song
I really do love my party
Luther, Luther
"I said I do Yeah
When are you gonna say
It's all right now?
It's all right
Ooh Baby"

Enveloped in song
Where are you?
I wonder

No, I don't!
That would be crazy
'Cause
you ain't say
you love me
Shoot!

Slow Poem

This is a
S
L
O
W
Poem
cause it takes a
L
O
N
G
time for people to get their
S
H
I
T
together sometimes
I watch with
P
A
I
N
trying not to let shit gain

M
O
M
E
N
T
U
M
in my thought space
Tryin' to be
E
A
S
Y
on this beautiful day
Wish all the bullshit would
F
A
L
L
like the leaves on New York trees
F
A
L
L

varying stages of what ain't good no more
down slow but not too slowly
S
O
M
E
T
I
M
E
S
it takes years
even for me
 to move
M
O
B
I
L
I
T
Y
ain't easy
overcoming is challenging
Something must be done
Can't always be "Easy on Sunday Morning"

P
I
C
K
yourself up
G
E
T
a move on it
N
O
W
slow motion ain't always good

What kind of shit is that?

          ____ told you what? Rock wit it   Oh Hell No!

Deal with it

          I love you Anyway! I just love him Got some Tya

I would have…

          What is it? He asked you what? That's grimy!

Sure did   Later for that shit   True That Be Easy Understand? Cut that out!

______ gave you what? Believe it   Oh snap! I didn't know   Tell it

Why? Oh no he didn't   I didn't say anything For real? Don't "F" wit me!

I'm scared of you! How could they   I don't get it   I just love her

Yes, they did!   Really? All jokes aside Truth   ___ off the hook!

A moment of clarity   Like lovely Lies   Handle it   Indeed

Seriously? No joke   I don't get it   Is that what you think? Oh shit!

What's up?   It is what it is   'bout time Oh no she didn't! Not my thing

You gotta be kidding   I love you mofo! Peace That's my baby!

I'm not playin'   That's some bullshit! That pissed me off!

Ain't got no kinda backbone!   Let it go   Splendid!
  You know what I mean.

Wow! I wish you would!   I can't wait!
  Payback   How we gon' do this?

Don't say nothing   Take it or leave it Cut it out
  Digame!

Dubious   I'm so sorry   Gimme love
  I miss you   It's all gone

I love that song   It's the real deal   "F" that!
  You know what you can do with that

And then some… And then some more.

Things Gone By

Tryin' not to be sad about things gon' by

Like

I got nothin' much of Mommy's 'cept

A crocheted orange and brown scarf and her long
skinny brown handled

Kitchen knife and a plastic rain hat she gave me to
wear on my head

"Put this on your head girl so you won't mess up your
hair!"

I been holdin' on to that plastic rain hat for a long
time.

Tryin' not to be sad about

Not havin' Mommy's house on Decatur

"I got this house so you all will always, always have a
place to go!"

Tryin' not to be sad

My one-bedroom apartment don't do nothing for my

Memories of Grandmama standin' at the top of the
stairs yellin' for somebody

Me or Mommy, or Ron, or Angie or somebody…

Jimmy or Donald or one of the little ones

Tryin' not to be sad about things gone by.

You Know The Rest

Came home

Had a shot of whiskey

Peach

In the name of love

That I lost

In the name of he can't love me the way I need to be
loved

In the name of I don't love you anymore

Hell…

I don't even like you

Really.

Came home

Had a shot of whiskey

Peach

In the name of bills and more bills

In the name of family shit

DRAMA!

I didn't mother you right---You say!

I didn't give you enough time --- You say!

I'm a bitch you say

Under your breath

Either way

I kept you and loved you and shared all the goodness I
was able to

Me and all my scars!

Me and all my scars!

Me and all my imperfections!

Came home

Had a shot of whiskey

In the name of I miss and long for and dream and
    desire and time gone by and right about now

I don't give a __________!

You know the rest…

I've done and will do the best that I'm able to

Because me and my scars and my joy and my pain and
    my songs of life and living and learning and hanging
    out made me who I am.

Came home

Had a shot of whiskey

Had a shot of truth

Had a shot of being with myself

And right about now, right about now

I don't give a ______!

You know the rest…

The Way It Is

I hope you're all happy
Happy in your loveless lives
your blameful lives
your unforgiving lives
I hope you're all happy
with your
days full of weed
no other way to exist
 it seems
nights filled with alcohol
no matter the kind
booze, beer…your liquid sunshine
lives full of lean
all the other substances you take in between
I hope you're all happy
being hurtful
being hateful
such destruction
war on self
war on peace
war on love
living in a made-up world
I hope you're all happy
in your loveless lives
pushing reality aside
thinking you're right

being unkind
hurtin' other peoples' lives
living in your mind
where the past thrives
emotional sickness
emotional hell – live there!
that's what you want
blame there
that's what you want
Just don't include me
count me out of
that space of anger and rage
that space of being unforgiving and unkind
no responsibility
no accountability
blaming – All the time
instead of appreciating or taking
one step at a time towards healing.
If that's how you're living
if that's what you want
There's nothing more I can say
Hurts to know that
this is the way it is

Intolerant

I will no longer tolerate your injustice anymore

I will no longer suffer from your ignorance and
  unwillingness to see the truth

I will no longer allow you to suffocate me with lies

You are choking me!

You have been stealing my history

Tearing families apart

Jailing my brothers

Raping Mother Africa

I will no longer tolerate your greed anymore!

I will no longer tolerate your writing my history, lying
  to my children, playing me cheap

While I sit and watch the profit you reap

For many have died and many are dying

In this never-ending struggle to survive

I will no longer remain locked behind your ignorance

To you,

Paper is more valuable than my life

Something that does not possess a breath, a tear, a
  smile, feel pain

I will no longer tolerate your injustice anymore

For I have seen the light and absorbed the truth and
  no longer will I remain the same

For a new day is coming and I must force you, force
  you to let me live in peace

Otherwise,

You shall have none!

I am emotionally in a place that I'd rather not be
Yet I summon all the strength that I know
From within and outside of me, to empower me
I need to do this when I'm low
Shoot!
I've been down low so many times and I say,
"Self, Keep going!"
I say, "Girl, keep it movin'"
I say, "Dag, I'm going and going and movin' and
    runnin' from what?"
At the end of the day, I say, "PAIN"
At the end of the day, I say, "HURT"
At the end of the day, I say, "REJECTION"
At the end of the day, I say, "AN EMPTY ROOM."
Shoot!
I keep it movin' and while I'm movin'
Memories are with me and every now and then
I'm able to hold on to one for a little while
One that makes me smile
Then, BAM!
Here comes all the ugly shit and I
Jump in the shower and I saturate my skin
With Lavender Vanilla or some raw Shea Butter
And I scrub my skin slowly
With a grainy, sandy mixture which leaves my skin soft
And for a few moments I get a reprieve

And I start to imagine good things, possible things
What if it were like this things
And I'm able to turn the water off and stand still.
I need to do this when I'm low
I need to summon all the strength that I know
From within and outside of me, to empower me.

Shoot!
I've been down low so many times and I say,
"Self, Keep going!"
I say, "Girl, keep it movin"
I say, "Damn, I'm going and going and movin' and
    runnin' from what?"
At the end of the day, I say, "SHAME"
At the end of the day, I say, "BLAME"
At the end of the day, I say, "DESPAIR"
At the end of the day, I say, "A WORLD FULL OF
    GLOOM"
Ooh, I keep it movin'
'Cause I know
The time I have to be still renders me powerless
Puts me in a state where heaviness lives
Right between my breasts
And I'm pulled into everything I can't stand
Stuff that makes me ache and cry and call for my
    Mama

Who is no longer here
Ooh, my eyes burn and, in my mind,
I see her!
Eyes full of promise, sitting unknowing
And then, I see her
Ooh, She's soooo cute!
And then, I see her
I remember the day I took that picture
Auntie always told me to smile
"Smile Baby," she said. "Smile for Auntie!"
And I did
'Cause I was happy and proud and feeling good!
Me and my seven-year-old self!
Happy and proud and feeling good!
Not too long after that
The world changed
And things I didn't know
I came to know
Things I didn't know
I was shown
Things I didn't need to feel

I had to feel
Things I didn't want to remember, I remembered
Talk about innocence taken too soon, TOO SOON
Sometimes I wonder

What things would have been like
If I hadn't had to grow up so soon.
I know I've been CHANGED!
I know I've been CHANGED!
There's so much stuff in the middle
Between then and now
Sometimes
I have to close my eyes
And allow the tears to fall
Warm water christens my face BECAUSE
There just ain't nothing I can do
There's nothing I can do!
That's when I have to flip and switch, or I toss and turn
Depending on where I am when the shit hits the fan
I know I have to dry my weepin' eyes
Pick myself up by those invisible bootstraps
And keep it movin'
There's so much stuff in the middle
Between then and now
In the forefront of my mind
Right smack in the middle of my day
And I say, "Self, keep going"
I say, "Girl, keep it movin' "
I say, "Damn, I'm going and going and movin' and
    runnin' TOWARDS WHAT?"
At the end of the day, I say, Brighter Days

52

At the end of the day, I say, Sunshine, Blue Skies
And gut-wrenching laughter
At the end of the day, I say, Possibilities
At the end of the day, I say, ALL THAT IS GOOD!
It is what it is
Was what it was
Would if I could
Ain't 'cause I can't
And I say,

Self
KEEP GOING
KEEP GOING
KEEP GOING
So many times, KEEP GOING!

Rivers Go On

My eyes are full

like a river that overflows

turning into streams

salty waters carry a residue of things that don't belong

As they pour,

I can see a little better

But the flow gets a little heavier

Then all the salty water enters the mouth of an
   existence

Suddenly

flooded with things that shouldn't have been in the
   first place

Drowning!

A constant stream of roaring wonder has taken place

And then the calm occurs

Warm sunrays penetrate layers of the unresolved

The way is so much clearer now

that my eyes are no longer full

like a river that overflows turning into streams

Upstream

   and

Downstream

no longer matter because as long as I can see and feel
   the sunshine sometimes

there will always be a way

Rivers go on…

Ghetto Shit?????:

Why it gotta be called, "ghetto shit?"
It's just the wrong shit
Ain't right shit
Livin' foul shit
Poor shit
No schoolin' shit
Who's rulin' shit
Wreckin' shit
Ain't teachin' their babies shit?
Don't wanna work shit
But want shit
Don't wanna build shit
But tearin' down shit
Don't wanna face shit
Erase shit, run shit
Escape shit
Some shelter shit
Misplaced shit
Why it gotta be called, "ghetto shit?"
How 'bout
Ain't doin' my part shit
Confused shit
Don't wanna be a loser shit
Don't own shit
Postponed shit
Delayed shit
Easily swayed shit
Made mistakes SHIT

Why it gotta be called, "ghetto shit?"

Child Of The Sixties

Child of the sixties
Where are you now?
Product of some broken aspirations
Martin Luther King's dream
Let freedom ring
And all that talk about we shall overcome someday
And the beat goes on.

Child of the sixties
Somehow, I see your face
Amongst the many distorted places
Those old tenements and those parks
with no swings and no dreams
NOT ENOUGH UNITY
NOT ENOUGH EDUCATION
Why don't you help clean up your block?
Don't you care?
I can make it better for you
Don't you care?
I can make it better for you
Don't you care?
About your baby,
brother or sister
mother
Are you a father?
Where's your friends?

I can't sleep at night 'cause I'm wonderin' if you gon'
  kill my mother
or my friend
maybe even me or my child
AIN'T NO STOPPIN' US NOW
Somebody shake me
Wake me when it's over
Somebody tell me that I'm dreaming
We are drowning in a sea of misery
Our children are being starved
malnourished in many ways
ROTTING!
Deprived of a mother and father
'cause they won't talk to one another
and be for REAL!
We're Gonna Be United,
I love you and you love me,
Then why are all our children
running around messin' up their minds
like nobody gives a damn?
Why don't they know they shouldn't throw things
out of the window
or hang out in those empty parks with no swings and
  no dreams
empty broken-down slums
That's where the children play in the summer

and in the winter, they hang out in cold hallways
gettin' high off whatever!
Somebody's bullshit
gets in the way of a child's
God given potential
You Better Get-Tough Kid
or those beautiful little babies
are gonna continue to die a slow death
like they're doing now
Their minds are being destroyed
Their creativity being stifled
As we
Search for Tomorrow
your grandma scared to go to the store or
ride the bus
'cause someone wasn't taught
 to respect themselves or other people
Somebody never learned how to change an ugly part
   of themselves
And we all have those
I DON'T GIVE A DAMN ATTITUDES
But when it threatens our very existence
When it threatens a baby's chance for some good
   things
In The Days of Our Lives
Wake Up Everybody

No more sleepin' in bed
The world has changed so very much from what it
   used to be
There is so much hatred, war and poverty
We Need We
in order to bring forth a brighter day
We're Gonna Be United
I love you and you love me
That dream
  that hope will become reality
When All My Children
learn to sit down and talk to one another
Be a Friend

When All My Children
strive to get what they want
without steppin' on somebody
Because
What goes around comes around
and if you think you're just gonna
Take—what somebody worked for
Get—without giving up something
Put a knife at my mother's throat
Take her rent money
While others lock up my baby brother
'cause he was born a color not preferred

Dogged them out, ragged them out, hung them out to
    die!

Mothers cryin', sisters cryin'

Ain't no lullabies being sung that much

"Hush little baby don't you cry" How do you not cry?

A people "keeping it real"

through all the pain and suffering continuous
    struggling

Doors closed from the onset

Someone builds ---You destroy

"Let freedom ring" ---"Justice for all"

Justice for whom? Just you!

You take and take

Deny and deny

Excuse and refuse

CONTINUOUSLY

While the wrongdoings and cutthroat actions are
    apparent

Televised even

You do what you wanna do

The laws are behind you and in front of you

Supreme Court Justice

A world wide situation---there's levels to this shit

Exploit and destroy

Manufacturing all sorts of things

Chemically insane and guns reign

Overuse

Bombard and bully with anything to gain dollars

Marvin said it, "Makes me wanna holler, throw up
both my hands!"

AI on the rise

'cause the human brain is no longer that important or
useful

Killing is so easy

Kill dreams, kill hope, kill compassion, kill!

Just wipe things out

Preference once again

Disregarding human life is what is done

Since this is the way it is and has been for generations

Very often change comes slowly and believe me

You will be rolling down the mountainside

One way or another

I'm gonna push you out

Blow you into another world

BY ANY MEANS NECESSARY!

You will live and die with all of those sick
motherfuckers

Who deprive us of our right to be human, to live in
peace

CUT THAT SHIT OUT!

Let's live---None of us are here forever

And now,

Now that you have had time

more than enough time
To think it over
When you start to change things
Look at yourself
Talk to those little people in your family
They need a guiding light
You see,
We have come to far to end it now.

Thought I would make it. Thought I would be quick enough to remove myself from his threatening gaze and his demanding words. Thought I didn't have to submit to his will because everything I had learned told me that I was free and had a will of my own. Free to make choices and free to make up my own mind. Everything I learned from Ma and Grandma during the past eighteen and a half years told me that I was not supposed to kiss anybody's ass. "You don't let nobody run over you," Mommy said. I was not supposed to let anyone threaten me and sit still. I was supposed to do something and somehow keep myself from harm. At first, I chose to speak up because I had something to say. Somehow, a difference of opinion became a fiery debate. It became so fiery and authoritative that my only recourse was to remove myself from the hot kitchen.

"Where you think you going?" He said. "I told you I ain't eating no pancakes for dinner."

"What's wrong with breakfast for dinner? Sometimes breakfast makes a good dinner.

I got outta class late, had to pick up the baby from my mother, plus I gotta finish my term paper! Damn, I'm tired Garrett!"

"Ain't no grown man wanna come home to no pancakes!"

"Well, grown man, Mr. Twenty-Year old. I told

you I got here late. I was rushing this morning and I forgot to take something out to cook before we left. You came home early G because I saw your bag in the living room. Why you ain't surprise me and cook something for a change?"

He was being difficult, and I was so annoyed. "Inconsiderate bastard," I thought.

I fed our daughter, bathed her, and sat down at the kitchen table doing my damn term paper. I was whipped! I didn't want to do the paper I had to do, and I had to get it done. I sure didn't feel like hearing Garrett's bullshit. But he kept on running his loudmouth, until I had had enough. I got up from the table and calmly said, "I'm going out for a little while."

"No, you're not."

"What?"

"You hard of hearin'? I said, No you're not."

"Huh? Why? 'Cause you said so?"

I replayed what he had just said. I knew and heard him clearly. I suddenly felt my insides drop to my feet and instantly thought, "He ain't gonna be tellin' me what I can and cannot do. Who in the hell does he think he is? He is not my father! This is bullshilt!"

His eyes were bulging out, wide open. I never saw him look like he did. I saw an eerie darkness coming out of them, and I saw his nostrils widen as he breathed hard.

"Go sit back down Cassidy! I ain't playin' with you."

He demanded that I do as I was told. Yet I made the choice, to proceed to the hallway closet to get my coat. My thoughts were on one track---Go out! His thoughts were somewhere else---Locked! There were two forces in opposition, each determined to have it their way. I had always thought and believed I was my own person. I was a homegrown replica of some of the strongest women in my family. With their images floating around in my head, I grabbed the doorknob.

"You better not walk outta this fuckin, house. I'm not playin' with you Cassidy!"

Choice. Homegrown freedom. I looked at him briefly and didn't say a word. "What?" I thought. "Watch me!"

He was standing next to the kitchen sink in his checkered boxer shorts, bare footed and bare chested. There was a plate of pancakes in his hands. I clicked the lock and snatched the front door open. Garrett dropped the plate on the floor! I ran!

There was quite a distance between the fifth-floor apartment and the street. I leaped from level to level, desperately trying to put some distance between us.

Quickly I jumped, feeling the burn of my weight in my ankles and feet. It didn't matter though because I continued to run. I had to get out of the building and get away from him! He was after me!

I ran, not knowing what to expect from the man who was chasing me bare footed, bare chested, and on cold stone steps in his underwear. He was so close behind me, one level, just fifteen steps away. He moved swiftly, faster than any person I had ever seen. I jumped those stairs, taking huge leaps until finally---I burst through the lobby doors and stumbled over the last three steps. Air! I felt the frigid winter wind explode on my face. I heard his feet pounding on the hard cement. I ran a short distance through the courtyard. He was just steps away. "Keep running girl, keep running!" I was horrified, horrified because when he leaped, he grabbed the collar of my rabbit coat and brought me down!

Oh my God! Before I was even able to think, he was dragging me back, toward the building, up the stairs. I screamed, "Get off me! Let me go Garrett! Let me go!"

He began punching me on the side of my head, on the top of my head. "Get off me, please let me go! Please!" I heard people lifting their windows and some were peeking through their blinds, watching. He yanked my body up two, up three stairs like the wheels of a shopping cart. There was a broken umbrella on the stairs. He grabbed it, without letting me go, and began slamming it all over my body for a few seconds. Before I knew it, he had broken the already broken umbrella across my arm. Tiring of that, he flung it. His blows were now landing all over my body.

"Stop, please…Wait!" I screamed. "Let me go, please…I'll go upstairs with you, I'll go upstairs with you!"

He shook and yanked me back and forth, continuing to drag and punch me. I was going up the staircase backwards, banging the base of my spine on every stair. I was part of diabolical shit that I never saw coming. He beat and kicked me! His tormented soul was released from a dark cavern of his own private hell. His eyes---I will never forget his eyes. They were deadlocked somewhere and void of all the love he had ever shown me. I was engaged with pure fury! His every strike, his every powerful blow was a blow against life and my spirit. Whatever I thought I was, was no longer. One right after the other they came and there was nowhere to turn without being struck. Suddenly, I blinked my eyes tightly. I don't know if I blinked them or if they were punched shut, but I know there was blackness, stars, and confusion in my mind. There was a rising heat on the side of my face. My top lip burst open at some point during the slaughter, and I covered my mouth. I was also trying to protect

67

my head. My coat had been shredded, along with my thoughts and beliefs. Finally, when we reached the top floor, I got up and staggered into the apartment, E4 fifth floor. I ran into the bathroom. He continued his tirade against my person for a few more seconds. Then he walked into the nearby bedroom, but not before saying, "I dare you to walk out the fuckin' door again!"

I fell into a corner behind the bathroom door. Oh my God, I was shattered! Oh my God, I was in trouble!

FAMILY POEMS

Meant To Be

(For Uncle Horace and Aunt Allie)

Early morning love
Had taken me on a journey
A journey to…
"The first time ever I saw your face"
You and a pretty lady.
"How sweet it is!"
How sweet it was!
Mommy and Auntie
Bloneva and Tootsie
Tootsie and Bloneva
Your big sisters
They sure loved you!
Ooh Wee
They said, "Look at my brother"
"Look at our brother"
Our brother this and our brother that
"Look at your Aunt Allie"
They admired them…Were proud of them
"Go on in there and talk to your Aunt Allie,
Go on in there!
A love that had taken us on a journey long ago
A love that has been there
A love that welcomed us

The "I ain't gonna let you down"
type of thing
The "Baby hold on tight"
type of thing
LOVE!
Wanting to be together
kind of love
The cryin' together
kind of love
The "I need you baby"
kind of love
Their love
Their struggle
Their ability to endure
Their realizing that they
Each had something
Beautiful to give
to one another
And to their children
And to their family
A union
A united front
ow sweet it is!

Us from up north
Us new people, new family long ago
Aunt Allie and Uncle Horace
And all their pretty brown babies
Derrick and Karen and Cassandra and Kim
All of those wondering eyes
Came to us
Came to New York City Ya know
To see us---Love, desire and wanting to know us
Love and family
Love and commitment
Love and struggle
Love and endurance
Love and dreams
Love and talkin'
About all the things that
MATTER!
"I love you and you love me" type of thing
We love you Aunt Allie
Here's to you…
Love
Early morning love
This morning
Had taken me on a journey
Yemi and I are here
'Cause we know

How sweet it was!
Loving by you
Ooh Wee!
The Minnie Riperton kind of thing
Lovin' you is easy cause you're
beautiful"
kind of thing
POWERFUL
RICH, STRONG
BLACK LOVE
UNITED! We're gonna be united
You and me
They said it 58 YEARS AGO
And they meant it!
As my mother would have said,
HOT DAMN!"
Here's to you…
We love you Uncle Horace

Just how important
You are in our lives
In so many lives
Aunt Allie, Uncle Horace
We love you! We love you!
HOT DAMN!
Here's to many more years to come…
A union, your union
Was meant to be
Was meant to be
Meant to be!

Ronay Ulay Fahlay

Mommy named him Ronald
Ronald Eugene Fairley
Then one hot, hot day
out of the blue
He stood before me
as I washed a sink full of dishes
And said,
"Girl, I changed my name!"

He was grinnin'
Beady eyes twinklin'
I looked at my brother like he'd lost his mind
"Get outta here Ronald," I said.

"No sister Dear!
You gotta hear my name
My name is like no other
It now has some PIZZAZZ
My name, the name of your little brother
Will make everybody GAG!"
So, with hot sudsy water all over my hands
I turned to him
He posed and said,
"My name
Is no longer that tired
Everyday people, same as my twin's

Our mother's bright idea
No reflection of me
No reflection of who I am

Can you understand that, Girl?
Can you understand that Sister Dear?

You just ought to
You who changed your name from Julie to Juteri to
What's that name your man gave you?
Qua-na-sia

Yeah
You stood on solid ground and told EVERYBODY
every single person you knew to call you
Qua-na-sia
I just said, 'Go 'head Girl!
Do your thing
I respect ya---Qua-na-sia'
Change
No more pork eatin'
Yip yappin' those lips with
Mommy's delicious pork chops
Ham sandwiches
Bacon
Bar-B-Q-Ribs

Ronay Ulay Fahlay

Spice ham and Cheese

'Cause it's a
Name thing
A
Change thing.

Now let's turn the beat around
Can you understand that?
I can understand that"

He stood before me
Beady eyes twinklin'
Remindin' me of what change means
"Everybody ain't gon' like it girl
But what that man say in Gone with The Wind?
What's his name?
Clark Gable
'Quite frankly my dear, I don't give a damn!'

I feel the same way Sister Dear"
And he had a smile on his face
Along with those beady eyes
Reddish brown freckles
Sandy brown hair
Size 13 feet

He looked at me
with all that he had inside and said,

"My name is like no other
The name I say of your little brother
The name I chose
And I like the sound,

Lookin' at me funny?
That's how you get down?
Well, I'm gonna tell ya
I'm here to stay

How you like this
Ronay Ulay?

Ronay Ulay Fahlay is me!

Look at your face,
See what I mean?

Like I said
And you heard that man,

    'QUITE FRANKLY MY DEAR, I DON'T
GIVE A DAMN!' "

He Was All That

(A poem about my big brother James Allen aka "Jimmy")

The lights were dim

in the house that was not ours

It was old and cold and lack luster

it reeked of smoke – coal burning

coming from the basement through the grate in the
floor

A burst of warmth was delivered sometimes

never enough to give us hot water

He always boiled it

to cook our food

or heat up what Mommy made

to wash the dishes

to add to a huge tin tub

that he dragged from the back porch

into part of the living room

near the warmth

His sister and little brothers needed baths

We were his priority when Ma was not home

She knew and she was always able to depend on him

to make the old wooden house a home

and he still had to do his homework

He was in Taft High School

He knew so much

made me read the newspaper aloud to him afterschool
before going out to play
made me say my multiplication facts
before going out to play
Needless to say
ain't have much time outside
Matter of fact
hardly any time out there at all
He always had something for me to do
clean paper was always nearby
time for me to copy
half the page of the newspaper
time for me to do it over
when it was not neat
He was my first teacher
A ten-year age gap made all the difference
had to listen to my big brother
he cooked good food
had to eat all my vegetables
had to eat the bread and butter that he served with
  dinner
I couldn't stand green peas
or bread and butter – I cried, he coaxed
And to this day
they are my least favorite foods
I watched him dance in the kitchen

The "Supremes" were one of his favorites
He listened to Classical Music
when washing dishes or during homework time
And to this day
I listen to Classical Music when I write
or simply need to think
He would practice his Baton twirl
for the Drum and Bugle Corps
I sat on the bed and watched or from the doorway
as he marched to a different beat
He took me places
saw my very first movie at the theater on Prospect
    Avenue
my first beach experience was Orchard Beach
and the New York World's Fair
Wow! So many people and that huge sphere
bus rides to Queens
He did that and then some
saw my first Off Broadway play
"Bye, Bye Birdie" – He was in it!
played the bartender
my eyes were wide open
as my cousins Terry and Jan sat nearby
I love Broadway and Off-Broadway theaters to this
    day!
He did so much for us

traced my foot on yellow lined paper

I didn't have decent shoes to wear to the store

He went down to Delancey Street

bought me blue leather shoes and some dresses

for the first day of school – fifth grade

and a little white seahorse to pin on my dress

And to this day

I love seahorses

He let me watch one TV show at night

on our floor model black and white TV

once a week for a little while with the covers tucked
under my chin

Ben Casey…Dr. Ben Casey

Man, woman, birth, death, infinity – the show's
introduction

I loved Dr. Ben Casey

he helped people – my first crush

And my big brother told me that

Dr. Casey would one day come see me

if I only went to sleep

I believed him

And I love medical shows to this day!

Man, woman, birth, death, infinity

He did all sorts of things for us – he was also very
stern

and he was not a saint

I saw him get angry
I saw him cry at the small white casket
 when our little brother Derek died
He did all sorts of things for us
supported, advised, gave money when he didn't have
     to
He was generous when he didn't have to be
I don't know how he did so much
 during his lifetime
He wanted to become more than our circumstances
He wanted us to become more than our circumstances
He helped me become a teacher
his friend Mr. Parker gave me an opportunity
to learn, grow and become instrumental
in the development of children
Over twenty-five years I remained
Big brother saw something in me
but not before saying, "Don't embarrass me!"
He didn't have to worry
I was grateful and wanted him to be proud
One day
his final day
as I was about to step out of his bedroom door
he said, "I love you, Julie!"
I knew he did
his actions throughout my life spoke volumes
Needless to say

to this day
and into "infinity"
I will always love my big brother
He was all that!

Auntie

Auntie

My mother's only sister

A wife

A mother

A grandmother

A great-grandmother

A good friend.

Bloneva Bernice, Mrs. Griffin, Ms. Applewhite, Blon

Auntie with the baad hats!

Auntie with the baad earrings!

Auntie rockin' her Tre'sor perfume!

Auntie with her Afrocentric self ---"Say it loud"

Auntie!

Full of splendor and grace

Full of elegance

She lived and she loved, and she was no nonsense

She was full of character and charisma

"Tell me about it…" she would say

An upstanding woman representing quality and
  goodness

Representing so much that was good

Auntie!

My Auntie

Summer after summer after summer

I became a Harlem girl

She sent Terry and Jan to pick me up from The Bronx
  – The last day of school

1390 5th Avenue became my home

Found myself into her world which was secure, safe
and full of love

Auntie gave me responsibilities --- I was ten

Opportunities to make some cash

"Jubu …Make sure you do a good job."

I took clothes off the line sometimes

I went to Sloan's Supermarket for cantaloupes and
yogurt

She loved them

And me

She watched me watch myself in the mirror

We laughed, "Jubu, You something else!"

There was nothing like hearing her gut-wrenching
laughter

I watched her get ready for work

She starched her nurse's hat…It was the brightest
white I'd ever seen

Just before she headed out the door, she'd say,

"See you later, Jubu…Be good.

Don't forget your money on the dresser."

She listened to my little girl stories

She listened to my singing

She listened to my mixed up, mixed match piano
playing

Never told me to stop makin' that noise

She just let me be me.

Auntie…

We talked on the phone

We ate out

We hung out on 86th street

She loved a car ride

She meant so very much to me

I learned about pride from her

"Pick your head up when someone is speaking to you,
Jubu"

She taught me how to wrap my first Gele

I wore it the first time I saw the Jackson 5

She called me "Gem…You're such a gem you know."

I knew she loved me, and I knew that I was special

Auntie loved her jazz!

She loved Nina Simone and Arthur Prysock and
Nancy Wilson and

Poetry

She loved life

The last thing she ever said to me was at a Daily News
Dance

I recited some poetry… Afterwards I walked over to
her table

She looked at me and simply said, "You did good Ju.
You are such a Gem."

I miss her.

Born Song

During the still of the night
Durin the rise of the early morning sun
Either way, I saw him
Either way, you saw him
Either way, one way or the other
Doing one thing or the other
Ooh, Baby, Baby!
And I hear his voice
And I hear his laughter
And I hear him singing his favorite songs
I see him dancing in the street
Or playing bongos on the roof or in the park
Sing Born!
"Here I Go Again"
And I hear him
"Over and Over Again"
All the while he, "Stayed in My Corner"
Our corners
Laughing with us through "Ebony Eyes"
Pinching our sides
Squeezing us tightly
And I hear his laughter
While begging him to PLEASE LET GO!
Silly
Silly of me to think that he would listen to me
He paid me no mind

He did his own thing

As he whispered plenty of "I love you," Quani

I knew he meant it

I knew he loved me, loved us ALL!

He protected me from harm

Jumped right in between me and hurt and pain

I'll never forget that

He protected me!

I do love you---BORN!

I do love you---WAYNE!

I do love you---BORN ALLAH!

I do love you, yes, I do!

As I see him in my mind's eye

Taking apart a kitchen stove and cleaning it
    thoroughly--- Picture that!

A teenage boy way back then cleaning a stove

While smiling and cracking jokes and preparing
    himself for his next adventure

Being around Born

"Sweet Harmony"

That's what Smokey Robinson sang

That's the song Born Sung, "Sweet Harmony"

Born sounded pretty good.

Born, Born Allah, Wayne, Suit Jacket Fred, Fatha,
    Uncle, Brother, Cousin, Best Friend

We are loving you
Will continue to love you
During the still of the night
During the rise of the early morning sun
I see you and feel you and will ALWAYS
Have you in my soul,
ALWAYS

Grandma

Grandma's hands went to work on Sunday morning
And Monday
And Tuesday
And Wednesday
And Thursday
Grandma was in a place often
Where she hadn't planned on being
And Friday
And Saturday
And on Sunday morning she prayed or she went to
    church when she could
God was always in her heart
She washed and she shopped, and she cooked tasty
    food
And she cleaned
And she hugged
And she kissed little hands
And she wiped snotty noses
Did what was necessary
She ain't have to do the extra, yet she did
Grandma shared wisdom
Grandma made mistakes
Grandma shared life lessons
She did her best when she didn't have to
Now, Ain't that lovin'?
Ain't that lovin'?

A Bronx Tale From 216th Street

I go to 216th Street,
863 to be exact
And
I always feel good.
Wanted
Appreciated
Love,
Nothing else matters.
They ain't even know me that long
Valerie,
Valerie Dash pulled me right in
863 is a major part of her foundation
And when me and her clicked,
She fit me right in.
Good vibes
Ain't no vibe unless Miss Ivy's included
She was the reason
Created more than a season
And loved a celebration just because
Life…She understood and let me in too
My task was framing two pictures for her
I made them special
Yes indeed,
I love them all!
I go to 863 E. 216th 'cause
Souls meet

Men and women, young and old
they understand life
and its riches
and all the bullshit too
and all the pain and sorrow that come with
being human
moving forward in some love and laughter each time
    we meet
is the way to go!
Doesn't mean things don't hurt
Doesn't mean they don't see shit
Everybody knows a tale or two or three
It's just that
some shit ain't important
ain't more important than being with everybody
Right Denine? Right Nene?
Miss Ivy's Queen,
A "hands-on" type of woman,
Orchestrating and demonstrating
Ain't no damn procrastinating
She says, "Make it happen" and it does
Everybody shows up to be with spirit
The spirit of love and unity and understanding
laughter reigns while music plays
Aw Shucks, the 863 in-house "DJ Chimere"
Got all the good music going on,

Chimere knows what time it is and how to get us going

Then comes Karaoke,

It's on and poppin'

Can't forget the "Soul Train" line and when "Footwork" comes on

Everybody gets their ass up! Everybody!

All kinds of food on the table

Tony's veggie lasagna and veggie ziti and meat balls

all fresh ingredients…Made with love

kitchen counters filled up, packed refrigerator

People coming in with all kinds of chicken, salads, cabbage, salmon, pizza, garlic bread, chocolate cookies, string beans, fried fish, baked beans, cake, macaroni and cheese

Oops, can't forget the drinky drink and that includes plenty of water

When you're inside 863, believe me

They let you in and let you know straight up

You matter

Yep!

And the spirit of all that is good is straight through the front door

I connect

863 East 216th Street

'Cause I matter when I am there,

Everyone matters.

863

For So Many Reasons

(A poem for Denise and Randy)

Talk about
there's no me without you
there's no them unless it's those two
Loving and kind
together
for the good and the greater good
Well-being is always on their minds
for themselves
 and others
Talk about
there's no me without you
there's no them unless it's those two
Two beautiful souls
Two beautiful people – entwined
Love is strong
a united front
There, when needed always
just ask anybody
giving their best
Randy all cool, quiet
reserved and determined
hardworking, dedicated
Denise on top of things
all the time

and that hearty laughter – Ooh Child!
that determined spirit – Don't be playin'!
Able to dance to the beat of her own drum
conga, tambourine, and many others
Along with that analytical mind – Oh boy!
break it down
She makes sure she gets things done
right
She makes sure
Loving
that's what she is
that's what they are
Caring
that's what they demonstrate
Talk about living and loving
Talk about building, learning and discovering
doing things to the best of their abilities
"Ain't no half steppin' "
when it comes to those two
Things are just right
Things are well done
Randy loves her
 just the way she is
and has no problem
 with whom she is
'cause sometimes she be loud

singing and laughing all over the place
he has no problem with who she is
That's important
That's beautiful
They do their best for each other
Their love lives and overflows
That's the way – That's the way they do things
Day in and day out
Most of the time
except when she says,
"Randy, gits on my last nerves! Bunk you Moody!"
They "Moody" each other all the time
"Moody where you at?" "Moody what you doing?"
Two Moodies
Of course
he looks at her
with eyes to the side – eyes wide open
lookin' at her like she CRAZY
and goes about his business
No matter the problem
No matter what it is
She blames him for everything
and guess what?
He pays her no mind
He loves her just the same.
And she loves him right back

Wholesome
Ready and sure
That's the way
That's the way they do things
All the time.

Snow. It is beautiful when it falls, and it lands on the limbs of the trees or when there is a narrow river nearby. All along the banks the new fallen snow has settled, its coldness resting on hardened soil. Later, when the weather warms, snow melts and tiny, microscopic elements become part of the soil. There is this whole grand scheme---the way I see things. One flake, one tiny, teeny, melted snowflake becomes part of a larger element, never to be seen as it was. Time and change. That is what it's about, isn't it? I once heard a man say, "Things change, but don't let the changes change you!" I thought that was some profound shit. Made me think. I started believing that no matter what, the essence of who I am, the core of my very being would stay intact. Deep.

So, when shit was going straight to hell all around, I was not supposed to change. My fun-loving, easy-going, hang-tough, go-with-the-flow self–dragged on through rivers of tears many a day–was not supposed to change. Through births and deaths, make-ups and break ups, addictions, divorce, newfound love, make ups and break ups, disappointments. Damn! I was most of the time; Redmon got to see me raw dog once. Hair all matted and plastered to my head; bedroom fucked up! Clothes are in piles all around the room. Old, dried chicken bones from last week sittin' on a plate on a dusty dresser. Ash tray full of cigarette butts, soda bottles on the floor. Ooh, the room was musty 'cause the windows were closed, except for one cracked just a bit. The rose-colored carpet had a gray tinge to it, and I did not give a good goddamn! I did not care that she visited me with the fine assed man she had been seein'. She was excited about him and wanted me to see him. Dayne was his name.

They entered the apartment, and I led them down the narrow hallway into my funky abode, leaving a trail of underarm stench behind. No skin off my back I thought. We chatted for a few minutes, and I got sick of myself and told them I was gonna go lay down. I cried after they left. Fell into crumpled, sweaty sheets and cried! Then rolled over and dried my weepin' eyes and kept it movin'. At some point in my mess, I got off my ass and began going through the motions, the whole try, try routine. Went into my bathroom and washed my face, stared in the mirror, looked around the bedroom, until I had drums beatin' behind my eyeballs, and Tylenol ain't work to ease the pain neither did Motrin. I laid back down, closed my eyes and rocked back and forth on my bed. Decided to call the damn HIP doctor and had to wait for him to call me back, so I would get the okay to come in to see my physician or any for that matter. Ain't that some shit? Did I need some motherfucker who didn't even know me to give me authorization to visit the doctor? That pissed me off! While I waited, I massaged my temples and stopped rocking. I had to see if the congas inside my head would cease, and I would get some relief. I needed relief from the recurring headache that surfaced every other week, along with a nagging nighttime cough. Oh, I almost forgot about my sore throat I had for two days---I managed to get over that with some good ole salt water and Listerine.

Damn, I better start takin' some Vitamin C and some multivitamins on a regular basis because I ain't no good right now. My job must be tired of me callin' in sick. I really don't mean to abuse things, but this is legit. I don't feel good! Whatever is going on with me this year ain't no bullshit; this is different. If this was back in the day, hey, I might have been partyin' too much and was recuperating when I called out. Or, if the love thing was just so damn good and I did not wanna leave him, then I probably woulda called out "sick." I don't do that shit anymore. I'm rollin' solo, by myself and right now, I am sick!

This headache is much worse than the others, and if that phone doesn't ring in the next five minutes, I'm going to the emergency room somewhere. Caledonia, Kings County, Downstate or Long Island University. It doesn't matter. I could have a tumor in my head. The scary thing about this is that there ain't nobody to call. "Tell the truth girl," I thought. I really didn't wanna bother anybody. Ain't nobody gon' really help me. Now why am I lying to myself? Truth is that shame and embarrassment got me in its grip as well. Damn, think another thought girl—Real quick! Okay, okay…I have a dream! Okay, what did the ancestors do out in those cotton fields and on those slave ships? Get up off your ass and move! Take a shower, do your hair, cry some more tears if you must, but get to gettin'!

In a moment of clarity, tears rolling down my face, snot runnin' out my nose, I rolled over and picked up the phone. Wasn't calling 911 or the hospital. I called my girlfriend.

"Hello, hello…Who is this? Mello, is that you?"

"Yes, It's me!"

"What's the matter, What's wrong? You don't sound right."

"I don't know girl…I just don't feel good."

Kinfolk

There is joy
a fulfilling of my spirit
right now, because right now
the possibility of me
seeing you all
is here,
Here!
In this lifetime
after all this time
I see the people who share
the same bloodline
we are defined
there is so much I have in mind
I know that I have family
kinfolk, relatives
cousins, cousins, uncles, and them
daughters and sons
nieces and nephews
babies and more babies
I am honored
I am ever so thankful, grateful
to share this time
this place and this loving spirit with you
family…my family
the blood of an African man enslaved
long ago was named Peter Page

who decided once freedom came

to change his name

to begin again

and the saga of the Applewhite family began

over a hundred years later

where it all began

in this land his family stands

then a relative of ours got a pen in his hand

Benjamin Jr. was his name, and he had a plan

He knew we had to know where we came from

AND

we've got to understand

This is special.

We must respect and honor those who came before

We must respect and love those who are before us
   right now

We must love one another --- FOR REAL!

No matter where you are

know that we are here

There are no excuses

we must do this

Family --- My family

The blood of an African man enslaved

long ago – His name was Peter Page

he decided, once freedom came

to change his name and begin again

Now on this day we'll do the same
because Peter's blood runs through our veins
and although we may have different names
never forget the place from where we came
from where we came
Reverend Peter Applewhite – I speak your name!
His wife Katie Applewhite – I speak your name!
Jacob, Isaac, Mike, Berry, Benjamin Sr.
I speak your names!
Sylvia, Eliza, Caroline – I speak your names!
Benjamin Sr. – I speak your name!
His wife Julia, their fourteen children
Emma, Lula, George, Lonnie, Sylvia, Cyrenius, Ganey,
  Sallie, Ada, Benjamin Jr.
Herbert, Caiphas (my grandfather) April, Julia
I speak your names!
These are the people
their blood in our veins
From where we came
I love you…
Kinfolk

Ronnie And Rosalyn

Ronnie and Rosalyn
Almost sounds like one name
especially because
you don't think about one
without the other
not in my view – those two
been together my whole life – seems like
two young crazy teenagers in love
a love that stems from way back when
two young crazy teenagers from Brooklyn
One gangsta'
One giddy
Ronnie ain't take no mess
and Rosalyn all goo-gooey,
lovin' her "teenage man"
She was always smilin' talkin' 'bout
Ronnie this and Ronnie that
Back in the day
a real back in the day when Dr. Martin Luther King
    was alive
Shoot, We ain't that old – just a reference point
to let you know just how far
Ronnie and Rosalyn been together
since forever
if forever is a thing
It is – We always say it when thinking about a long
    time

Forever and a day, you know – whatever that is
That's what they is
That's what they are
A dynamic duo
Way back days and way back nights
all those times when money was tight
No place to go but to sleep in each other's love
with dreams put on hold
in each other's hustle – the scramble
The "We gon' make it through this shit!"
Even though, "He git on my damn nerves!" She said.
Even though, "She git on my damn nerves!" He said.
"I still love you though!" He said.
And then there was laughter and slow music and game
    nights
and lots of loving each other
Been together since forever
if forever is a thing
Their thing being "Let's Stay Together"
"Can This Be Real?"
That's what he sang – That's what he sings to his main
    squeeze
in a living room full of people
Ronnie loves that song!
Together
Ronnie and Rosalyn

during the highs and the lows
How low can you go? They know.
How high can you reach? Way high
if high is a place – They know.
Been there, done that
Along with the five they created
Plus, one… Yes Chevette, you are part of it too!
Insuring that forever and a day thing will go on and on
Lots of them now
Love keeps growing
Been together since forever
if forever is a thing
Ronnie and Rosalyn
Love! All the way love
way back love
today love
Simply beautiful

LueVada

Been so many places
In my life and time
So many places
During this life of mine.

"Every woman whoever loved a woman,
You ought to stand up and call her name."

LaVeda, Veda, Mommy, Grandma, Mama

During this life of hers
She'd seen so many things, felt so many things
She'd spoken to so many people
Welcomed them into her heart, into her home
Wherever she was…
"Hey there Sugah! How you doing Baby?"
That was her way, you know, Veda's way.
"Come on in and sit down while I shuck this corn
make some spaghetti and meatballs for y'all
go on in there and turn the TV on
play some music.
Hey Sugah, What's the name of that song?
can't be with the one you love,
Ya gotta love the one ya with Sugah!
That's right Baby, love the one ya with!"

We laughed and had a good time.

Time went by and days, weeks, and months
Turned into years
Years brought change
Change brought tears
She welcomed me into her heart
Into her home
'Cause I was all broke down, from a dirty low down
She let me sleep peacefully
And afterwards she fed
Then "Jenny Baby" did my hair.

Veda was a bad go getter
Shake a mean low down
Take a little bit of nothing and could turn it around.

"Every woman whoever loved a woman
You ought to stand up and call her name."

LaVeda, Veda, Mommy, Grandma, Mama

She let us all in
Into her heart, into her home
Living and loving and sharing and laughing and
    talking and teaching us lessons.

ROCK STEADY!

She let us all in,
Girlfriends and boyfriends, cousins, and then some
She loved us all and simply let us be
"Be good, Sugah! Be good."

Been so many places
In this life of mine
So many places, and through her I could see
There was no one who did things quite like her.

"Every woman whoever loved a woman
You ought to stand up and call her name."
Mommy, sister, daughter, grandmother

LaVeda, LaVeda, Veda!

118

Miss Thompson

(A poem for Sallie on her 50th birthday)

I'm gonna take this back
To a time and place
About 51 years ago
Ooh, what did I say?
Doesn't seem that long
Though things did change
But for many of us
They remain the same.

Girl,
You still have the same smile
And that sparkle in your eyes
Same pretty face
And the coolness in your stride
Same sounding laughter
Slight mustache above your lip
You always had it going on
You were always so equipped.

Being with you was easy
'Cause you were always
Just so cool
And you could dance and really do your thing
And it was always nice and smooth.

Remember…

We were standin' outside

On a warm, summer day

The music came from somewhere on 183rd Street and
Ryer Avenue

Suddenly, we heard the Jackson 5!

"STOP THE LOVE YOU SAVE MAY BE YOUR
OWN,

GOTTA TAKE IT SLOW,

'CAUSE SOMEDAY YOU'LL BE ALL ALONE!"

Girl, you started dancin'

That dance we were doing back then

We all joined right in

Then we laughed and had a good time.

Ooh!!

There was this other song

You used to sing

It was a big hit back then…

"DRY YOUR EYES,

THERE IS NO NEED TO CRY

SO LONG…"

So long,

We'll meet again!

That's what I said and me, you, Bonnie, Valerie, and
    Wanda
Stood on 183rd Street and Grand Concourse and cried
After I said somebody's poem
On a bright sunny day
The day after ninth grade graduation
Not knowing the depths of "We'll meet again!"
That was 1969.

Girl, Time…
Ain't it funny how time
Just
Slips right on away.

Doesn't seem that long
Though things did change
But for many of us,
They remain the same
You still have the same smile
And that sparkle in your eyes
Same pretty face
And the coolness in your stride
Yeah Girl
I gotta tell you
I love ya!
I love ya!

Last Words

by Ronald Eugene Fairley

We go through a lot of stuff in life
Ups again, downs again
Time again, time again
Ups again Baby
When a child is born, we can say
that is a new beginning of a new time
Is that real time?
Thinking of the beginning of time
When there was no light
Only the stars, the Earth, the winds, and the rains
The hot and cold weather
Ups Baby
Talking about the beginning
The beginning of time
Not when you wake up in the morning and open your
  eyes
But the beginning
The real beginning
"As it was in the beginning, it shall be in the end"
We all will meet up
In time
Real time
Peace and love
To all things on Earth
Yes, all things my friend

Hot Buttered Soul

(A Poem for Mr. Paul Koonce Sr.)

I had sunshine
On cloudy days
'Cause he could fix
Anything!
His brown skin
Was pretty and he glistened in the sun
As he strolled by on any given day
Daddy,
He was a rolling stone
Papa
He loved a big Christmas and farm life
Country living was his thing
He had a way about him
Made you smile
Kept it real
Talk about tell it like it is
You could smell…breathe in…Old Spice or the soft
  scent of Jergens lotion
Clean and cool as he strolled by
Rocked his pipe
Kept it with him
Paul with the pipe…
Dad was smooth
He loved nice clothing

It all fit---head to toe
And women…You know the rest
Daddy loved women
Beauty---He loved beauty---Differently---Quality
And he gave and he worked hard and did his best
He could fix anything
As he drove through life
Not perfect, yet better than most…He dreamed!
He could fix anything!
Even a child's hunger for one thing or the other
His change in a jar,
For us
Paul with the pipe
Clean and cool
Clean and smooth
Daddy
Loved to talk and tell stories
Giving us all an education of sorts
His way
His truth---he kept it real
Daddy gave and worked and dressed and loved life
   and did the best he could
Sunshine…Hot buttered soul
We had sunshine on cloudy days…
Sunshine, son shined
He kept it real…
Paul, Mr. Koonce, Daddy, Brother, Cousin, Friend
Hot buttered soul!

Jenny Baby

(A poem for Jeanette on her 50th Birthday)

Oh girl,
I'd be in trouble if you left me now
I'd be in trouble if you left me now
"Sure would." She would say.

The first time ever I saw your face
Fifty something years ago
On a summer day
You were lookin' out the window
I was sittin' on a car downstairs
I looked up,
You said, "What's your name?"
I said, "Julie"
You said, "Well, Come on upstairs Julie"
And I did.
I became "Juliegirl", and the world changed.

From that day on, going to Jeanette's house became
    part of my daily schedule. I couldn't even go to the
    store for my mother without stoppin' up there.
Day and night
Rain or shine
Saturday mornings watchin' "Soul Train"
Playin' Hookey and eatin' your steak and corn

Plain ole "chillin"
Talkin' 'bout
This or that
Who is doin' who and who's hair is wack

Oh girl,
I would be in trouble if you left me now
If we weren't chillin'
You would be doin' my hair
Gettin' us ready to be in the street somewhere
Goin' around a corner
Or…
Downtown on a train
Goin' to some party
Then right on home again.
We would laugh and laugh and have a good time!

Then before we knew it
Real life was upon us
Along with babies, boyfriends, and responsibilities
And sadness, loneliness, and heartaches and long-lost
    dreams
I did not see you for ten years
Yet during that time
You crossed my mind
Over and over again

And in 1983
You and me
Saw each other again.

Real life was upon us, and I was on the move
I was feeling bad
I was feeling low
Hair all matted to my head
You said, "Come on Girl, let me comb your hair"
I did
And I sat still
Eyes closed
And told you what was in my heart and my soul and
  your eyes
Filled with tears
I was able to just breathe
I knew then that you were truly my friend
All those nights that I could not sleep
All those nights when I tossed and turned
I would pick up the phone
You talked to me for hours and sometimes daybreak
  would greet us.

I needed that Jeanette,
Thank you for putting the ground back under my feet.
Thank you for being there every time I needed you

Feeling my joy and my pain
Feeling the laughter again and again and again.
Jeanette…My sistah!
My sistah!
You know I love you, right?

LOVE POEMS 129

Love That Is...

I want love that is wholesome
nurturing
beautiful
reciprocated
enduring
encompassing
sure.
I want love that wants me
needs me
loves me
honestly
in the long run.
Ain't no half steppin'
Ain't no forgettin'
about us
no matter what
We come first
We come first
Wholesome and sure.

Girl
I couldn't sleep 'cause I was worried
about ya,
Wonderin' whether I would ever go shoppin'
with ya,
and wonderin' whether
We would still be
The same friends…
And remember the time
You and I played in the street?
I threw popcorn in your hair
And you called me a stupid bitch!
We laughed and had a good time.
Remember that Christmas we wanted those leather
  coats
with the wide belt that stretched from side to side
Two toned leather coats
We thought those coats were baaad
And we didn't have a dime to buy one.
I begged Granny to buy my coat
You and I did everything we could to buy yours,
From babysittin' to robbin' your drunk stepfather
We got our coats and were happy
laughed and had a good time.
And then there was the time you were mad at me
'cause I tore your socks

We didn't speak for a whole week
But I knew you cared about me
And if we could laugh about me
throwin' popcorn in your hair
We would still be friends
Damn,
I was happy when next week came
and so were you.
Now
the years have gone by
We have children
Who happen to be first cousins
'cause somehow
We fell in love with brothers
and once again the bond of friendship we had
grew stronger
Since I didn't have a sister
I figured now I would call you my own.
We still got mad at each other
cursed each other out
acted as though we didn't care
Walked around not speakin' and seein' each other for
   a long time
But then we did,
   And
         we
             had

a good time.
Now I'm sittin'
In the emergency room
Waitin', hopin' and wonderin'
Will my sister
        be alright
Wonderin' if I would still be able
to call you at midnight and you be there
so we could talk about
Sometimes, nothing important
And it didn't matter
Because we cared…
But now,
My girl hardly knows me
Due to pressure, due to strain
She's here in body
And while I'm watchin' my best girl
I'm lookin' through an empty shell
Wonderin' why life is cruel
to so many people who love life
And
I'm wishin' that when you wake up tomorrow
I could throw popcorn in your hair
Hear you call me a stupid bitch
go shoppin' and have a good time.
Girl, I love you!

Maybe Tomorrow?

If ever I could have showed you
For so long I wished I knew
Some way to relieve the heartache
That we have been going through.
For so long I searched for answers
Many times, we lost our way,
All our dreams for tomorrow
Have slipped away,
Have slipped away.

I see you in my mind, Baby
laughing, crying, sighing
Holdin' me
Lying
talking all sorts of crazy shit
and looking good in the morning sun.

Early morning love
had taken us on a journey
Stay in my corner!
Stay in my corner!
Brought tears to my eyes
We stood as one
Unclothed in the morning sun
Bared our souls to one another
and cried real tears.
Never knew love like this before
Maybe tomorrow?

First Sunday In August

The park
was crowded
and the people
moved
smoothly, continuously
one way or another
drums echoed in the distance
little children shot long streams of water
at one another
until they were
soaking wet
Tee shirts sagging and clinging to warm
souls
All kinds of flavors
All kinds of smells
Folk
black, brown, red
All over
The drums played
I saw
him, her, them
The park was crowded
movement
crossing paths
passing by
People

Crotona! Crotona!
it was hot

it was jammed

in the distance
I told you I saw them
I told you it was crowded
babies
new babies
old
old school
Say what???
new and old
Say who???
Yesterme
Yesteryou
Old school flavor
Do it 'til you're satisfied
Old school
Old timers
The park was crowded
all over
The people moved
right
into
my
heart!

Men can be really inconsiderate
And I'm being nice.
You can
cook their food,
have their children
clean their "drawers"
set aside dreams.
Massage their feet
Support their endeavors no matter how far fetched
You can walk their dogs
Rub their aching backs and stroke their b- -s
You can Daddy this and Baby that
I ain't never like nothing in the crack of my a—
But I wore a thong.
I'm flat footed
Wore heels even when they hurt the fourteen year
old corn on my left foot
Oh, the requests made
Do this, Baby
Oh, not like that
Come on – Let me put it in the back
Girl – I ain't gon' hurt you
Baby – Cosign for this
You ain't gotta worry about nothin'
I got you; I love you
Baby, you took it the wrong way

It wasn't like that
She ain't mean nothing to me
It just happened
I ain't never gon' leave you!
Don't be like that
We can work it out.
I'm sorry, Baby
You know I love you, right?
Look at me, girl!
Hold me
Love me Baby
Baby, would you pick this up for me?
Meet me over there
Baby, Baby
I don't feel good.

The Way Home

They say that
home is
where the heart is
Since this is what I've come to know
come to realize
I
just couldn't stand it when I
one day
found myself
far, far away
lost! lost!
far, far away
There was me
There was me
In a world full of endless possibilities
And all the dreams I ever had
All the endless possibilities
far, far away from me
I
just couldn't stand it!
just couldn't stand it!
Deeper and deeper
All the while
in my heart
I knew I had to
Had to find my way

Had to find my way
My heartbeat and beat and beat
I just couldn't stand it!
Didn't understand it!
Yet, I knew and believed
Home is where the heart is
A place where
mind, body, and soul
you know
Have a love connection
A love thing going on
Had to
get back to the dreams
Had to get back to my heart's desires
Had to
turn around
look where I was going
Every step of the way
Eyes wide open
Bumped into and landed on
roads not traveled
The tears fell, the heart ached
The heart ached, the tears fell
I kept moving freely, FREE!
There was nothing EXCEPT
A power

Greater than me
Along with my will to be
Along with my will to go home
HOME
The place where mind, body and soul
You know,
Have a love connection
You know,
A love thing going on.

Today,
I am home!
I am able!
I am Free!

My mother passed away quite some time ago and one
morning, not too long ago, I woke up with a vivid
memory of her. When I was about ten years old,
my mother would put her music on, sip her Johnny
Walker Black and play two songs repeatedly! I would
watch her from a room in the house and be MAD!
Ooh, I was sick of those songs. Why would she keep
playing them? However, that morning, with that
memory, I longed for her. I needed to feel her, and I
needed something tangible, right then! I got dressed,
drove downtown to J&R Music World and just waiting
for me was Gloria Lynne's Greatest Hits. When I
arrived home and put it in the CD player, I closed my
eyes and stood in the middle of the living room floor.

If you ever get the chance, YouTube the songs, "I Wish
You Love" and "I'm Glad There Is You." I want you
to feel "My Mother, The Woman." Many years later,
I understand why she played them. The poem will
convey so much of what it means to live and to love.

My mother, the woman
Filled with desire
Filled with passion and pain
Filled with tears.

My mother, the woman
Filled with love
Filled with tenderness
Filled with dreams.

My mother, the woman
Showed me, told me
How to love
How to treat love
And how to let love go when need be.

My mother, the woman
Said I was her queen
And that means
I was royalty in her eyes
Even when I couldn't see it.

My mother, the woman
Sang songs of pleasure
Sang songs of life
Sang songs of truth

All of which was heard
Through piano keys
Black and white
Cut and dry
Thick and thin.

Yeah,
My mother, the woman
Lives in me!

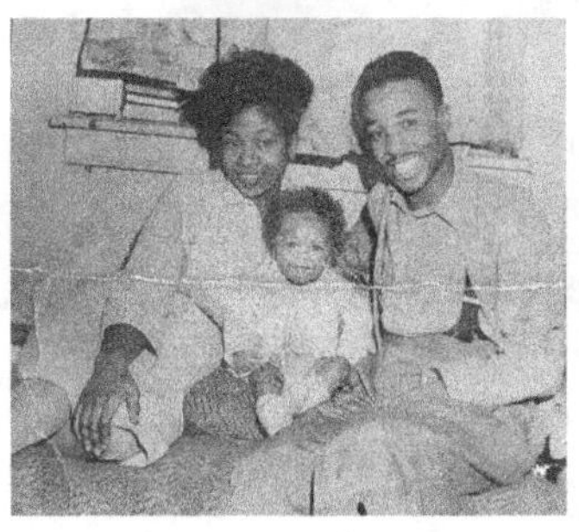

Anyway

Daddy,
I loved you from the very beginning
When I realized I was me
There was you
'Cause Mommy said so
I loved you from the very beginning
And even though
You never called me
My dreams included you
My life stories included you
And I had pictures in my mind
Of all the possibilities of you and me
Once, I imagined you watchin' me jump rope
Once, I imagined you takin' me shopping
Once, I imagined you coming to my school
And once, I imagined you
Picking me up and wiping my bloody face after Lenny
Accidently
Hit me with the baseball bat
Pictures in my mind
All the possibilities of you and me
Daddy
I loved you from the very beginning
When I realized I was me
Listening to all of Mommy's once-in-a-while stories
    about you
I felt good, anyway…

My Daddy,
Knows there's me
My Daddy has to be
Busy
Busy
And even though
You never sent me a birthday card
And even though you missed every graduation
And even though
Andre Bennett beat the daylights outta me in the
  schoolyard
And even though
Melvin gave me a black eye and took my money
My hopes for tomorrow included you
My prayers for better days included you
And I had pictures in my mind
Of all the possibilities of you and me
Once, I imagined you telling those wild boys not to
  bother me
Once, I imagined you at the cookout
Once, I imagined you cookin' breakfast
And once, I imagined you pickin' up the phone to call
  me
Pictures in my mind
All the possibilities of you and me
Daddy
I loved you from the very beginning
Anyway.

This Is My Luther Poem

(For all those who know Luther Vandross)

Superstar, it's
Forever For Always
You
Give Me the Reason
Love Won't Let Me Wait.
Anyone Who Had a Heart
Wouldn't find a Better Love
You're
So Amazing!
Don't you remember
you told me you loved me
Baby
Superstar,
It's Forever, For Always
You
Give me the reason
You're
So Amazing!
Since I
Lost my
Baby
Superstar
It's Forever for Always
You Give Me the Reason

Don't you remember?
Don't you remember?
Don't you remember?
Superstar
If This World Were Mine…
Superstar,
The Power of Love
 I Love You
Forever For Always, For Love.

All There Is To Love

Lover
of warmth and tenderness
Hear my cries!
Hold me with burning desire
make me smile
Free me
from cold and emptiness
Suck me in
Dry my tears
Kiss my face
Moist hands are gentle
Strong hands are smooth
Stroke my thighs!
Like the sun
burn me up!
Blow warm breezes in my ears
Lay me down and call me Baby
Feel my heartbeat
embrace my soul
Touch me tenderly and let me taste
All there is to love
It will be easy

Blue, Royal Blue

Never thought it would come to this

The place where each bedtime is laced

with the echoing-----sounds of a train passing by

Or swooshes of moving cars every now and then in
  the wind

Just outside my window

the night-----its darkness awaiting

My mind is out there and inside a bedroom

where no one ever awaits me

I tell myself each day

I am woman---I am woman!

Hear ye, Hear ye,

Be all that ye can be!

It's cool---It's all right

Ain't no fella gotta be here or me be there---with him

Entwined

Arms and legs, fingers, and hairs and toes and lips all
  wet and sopping up

each other's desires

Naw,

I don't need that shit no more

Naw,

I don't need to hear his laughter and his breathing and
  his explaining and his

passing gas or his singing

Naw,

I don't need to see his shiny, smooth body
Skin like silk
Muscles all big and bold and him smelling so damn
    good!
Naw,
I don't need to see or feel warm hands
against my skin
against my thighs
against my face
Or feel his big head in the fold of my arm and me
    lovin' it
Naw.

The frigid temperature made walking to the subway seem farther than usual. Cold winds blew briskly while the leaves rode the air high and low. Sudden gusts were so powerful, people walked with their backs toward its impact. The awnings on many storefronts flapped in unison, ceasing only as the winds calmed down. The air was fresh, entering the nostrils like a swift whiff of Vick's medication.

I rushed out of my apartment with no destination in mind; none other than I was going to The Bronx. I knew that the long Brooklyn ride would give me time to think about my entire life, my job prospects and absorb the world around me. I was ready to take anything. I had been unemployed for over a year, after working in the New York Daily News Circulation Department. It was a year too long. I took classes at the Brooklyn Adult Learning Center to freshen up on my typing skills. I couldn't just sit around the house and watch television every day or be chit chattin' with Lenora over coffee. That shit was never part of my damn dream. I had to get out of the confines of my bedroom. I was shrinking in there! I told anyone who called that I didn't feel well. Either it was a headache or a backache. Sometimes it was a toothache or a stomachache. When I called Denise, I even told her I had an ass ache. She laughed, but I wasn't joking. My entire life hurt. It all balled up into one thing; things were taking too long to happen, and I was tired of the struggle. My behavior was indicative of a soul that was pressed. Pressed against unfulfilled dreams and the problems of my world. Both summoned me with equal force each day. I had stayed in bed for days. My heavy black jeans and sweatshirt made moving underneath the comforter difficult. I laid amongst scattered clothes and other clutter, knowing damn well that was wrong. Every now and then I stared at the floor. The rose-colored carpet was stained with Pepsi Cola and coffee. Cigarette ashes and match stems had fallen out of the ash tray. I'd left magazines, an empty plate and a cup on the dresser, along with the things that belonged. There was a Holy Bible on one end and a Holy Quran on the other, in addition to my Serenity Prayer. The prayer had been printed on a big brass plate that sat there as well. For quite some time, all I had been able to do was lie down, let the music play from the radio near my bed and sleep. Yet there was something different about this day as I whispered the Serenity Prayer. Most of the time, I read it, unable to internalize the significance of the words. It was different now, at that moment. "God grant me the serenity to accept the things I cannot change, the courage to change the things I can, and the wisdom to know the difference." My legs had gotten tangled within the covers on the bed and with sudden jerky movements, I yanked them free. I rolled over and placed my head on a cold pillow, stretched my arm out and brushed away the grit on the sheet. "Get your ass up and out of this bed, girl! You know better than to wallow in shit, don't lay in despair. Find a way out, now!"

All I could think of was the fact that I needed health benefits and a steady income to support myself and my three teenage girls. Child Support was only two hundred and fifty dollars a month and the rent was five hundred and seventy-five. I ain't have no time to be choosey. I was just glad that I had gotten my

bachelor's degree to help me along the path. I also knew I would need typing skills to help me when I got ready to go get my master's degree. I had dreams and I had to do my best. In no way was I going to let the ancestors down. How could I not excel when they had so much less? How could I let my mother down? How could I disappoint myself? I did not want to carry that burden. I had to get outside myself and my thoughts. Period! In doing so, it meant going to visit the place I knew and anyone that I meant something to. I needed to feel love.

On my trek onward and out of the pits, I quickened my pace down Rockaway Parkway when I saw Ms. Nunez in the distance. "Let me help her back to the building before I go uptown," I thought. She struggled with a shopping cart full of laundry and a shopping bag full of groceries. She stumbled when the wheels hit the broken pavement. I watched her pick up some clothes and a large bottle of detergent that had fallen. She was flustered. The scarf around her neck was flying one way and her no button coat another. Mrs. Nunez had five big children, ranging in age from fifteen to twenty-five. They were always running around the neighborhood. I could not understand why they seldom helped their mother. I could not stand the way they treated her! All that lady did was work, work, and provide for them. The three oldest seldom went to school and they did not work. One or the other was dropping in and out of college. They were often outside the building talking to their friends about what they were into; "I'm an artist and I got skills. Gonna open me up a studio." Another one, Jackie said, "I'm in the studio making tracks and I'm Rappin', my shit is dope." Each time I saw them, they were always puffin' on something. Their eyes were all red, swollen and squinted. They were always singing the same ole song to one another, "I'ma be this and I'ma be that." I watched them grow older. I saw them during my comings and goings throughout the years. I saw their mother become weary and haggard. I helped Mrs. Nunez anytime I could though and thought, "They will be sorry one day."

I rushed toward her and shouted, "Hey Lady, Lady! Give me that bag right now!"

"Oh Celeste," she said with a huge sigh. "Don't bother, I can make it. I'm almost there."

"I know you can make it, I'm just gonna make it easier," I said with a smile on my face. "How about that?"

She allowed me to take the bag full of groceries and I also grasped the shopping cart, pulling it with her. I wanted to do all that I was able to do at that moment, if only for a few steps. She didn't fight me on it either. Ms. Nunez simply said, "Gracias Chica, Thank you mi amor. You are such a good person, you really are."

We reached 1625 and I walked her inside. I hurried toward the elevator as other people were exiting and held the door. We said our, "See you laters," and I resumed my walk down Rockaway Parkway. I ain't gonna lie; it felt so good to be outside feeling that freezing wind against my face. I only had carfare and three dollars to my name. At the same time, I had a mother, girlfriends, brothers, and a professor from college that I respected and dreams that needed to be fulfilled. I just had to tell myself some different things that made sense. I realized that I had made some messed up decisions and that life was not fair. I also believed some beautiful life was ahead of me. Fight the feelings, cry the tears, and talk about my issues. Somebody out there, somebody in my circle knows a lot more than me. Somebody would lead me out of my personal abyss.

It's A Small Thing

Old, worn out
Broken
but it still stands
I want it 'cause it was hers
Paint chipped
drawer missing
sanded it down
scraped it
'cause somebody along the way
decided to
put white semi-gloss paint
on the wooden structure long ago
white paint and dripping wet things
were put upon it and someone wiped the wood
over and over again
I sanded it down
wiped and soaked the old wooden structure
in paint remover
scraped and scraped
until frustration changed
Everything!
Then the piece was
immersed in water
frustration changed Everything,
Everything!
Ever smell wet, wooden furniture?

Now the wood has come apart in places
Lifted up
chipped paint along the four legs
cracks
lots of cracks on what Mommy claimed long ago
The now brown slashed spotted slashed chipped
    slashed
scraped slashed dipped in a tub of hot fuckin' water
to get the damn process going bathroom table
Ain't worth a thing
EXCEPT to me
It's a small thing
Old, worn out
Broken
But it still stands
It still stands.

Am I Just Another Bitch Who Ain't Shit?

You know

I ain't gon' tell no lie

I'm sittin' in this kitchen chair

Lookin' outta my window

Tryin' to act like

things ain't botherin' me and I know they are

'Cause I hurt someone I love and care a lot about and
  now they're hurtin' me back

I'll tell ya,

It doesn't feel good

I know something ain't right

And maybe

Ya feel

That I ain't shit

You don't like me no more

'Cause

I shouldn't have done what I did

And now

you gon' act like you and me and me and you are still
  all right

on days that you feel like it

And you think that I don't know you're angry at me for
  somethin'

Girl…

We got through some emotional hell

And we were there for we

And I'll never forget how you made me see

Showed me another way
And I thank you
Sounds silly maybe
'Cause I did somethin' to you
And now you figure if you are stink with me
That we'll get somewhere
And maybe
You don't care
Just another bitch to you
All that we done seen together
Can't be make-believe
It was real
And that's why
My silly self
has to sit down and show her real self to you
And if you and me were ever really for real
Being our different selves
Our place
in the human family
will be all right again.
Now maybe
I'm the only one who feels anything
And you don't care one way or the other
Maybe I'm
just another bitch
who ain't shit
'Cause now we're seein'

a different side to one another
And it ain't good
But me and you said one time
Everything ain't always good
Gotta take the good with the bad
And the bitter with the sweet
If you care about something or someone sometimes
But if you don't care
These words don't mean a thing
And we both
Walk away from one another
Feeling bad
Tryin' to stuff it off
'Cause we know
Life goes on
And somehow, we will always wonder
About one another at some time
I ain't gon' tell you no lie
This is me
And if me and you
Was ever really for real
There is another side of me
Who makes mistakes sometimes
fucks up
laughs, cries, sighs
Am I just another bitch who ain't shit?

Could It Be?

I was sitting on the train
wondering whether
loving someone
would be as easy
as it was before.
Unexpected romance
how good it feels
especially when you both are
feeling it at the same time
Gentle and warm
Soft and sweet
My mind entertains succulent
moments with you
Each moment sweeter that before
Seconds later
wanting you for more…
Funny
'cause I don't know why
I feel this way.
I'm tickling you in my mind
with moist fingertips
My slender legs wrapped around
Someone so
Indescribably delicious
One day
I'll devour you

doing a thorough job
leaving scents of soaking wetness in the air.
Thank you for being
who you are and there for me
Guess loving turned out better
than it could ever be
Could it be?

Just Because

I wanted to hold him
Lay my head across
his shoulder and close my eyes.
I wanted to feel him
Rub my hand against his neck
and feel his thigh.
I wanted to be with him
Look into his face and see him smile.
I wanted to love him
Just because he is
A man of mine!

Lovin' Is…

(A LaShon, Eyhana, and Ilasia poem 1984)

Lovin' is
    Gentle and sweet and
    Soft and warm
    Skinny and ugly and
    Black and white
    Bread and water
    Mommy and Daddy
And stayin' over Aunt D's House!

Lovin' is
    Dyin' and cryin'
    Buildin' and baking bread
Lovin' got a roof over Grandma's head
Lovin' helps me out!

Lovin' has me talkin' to you
Standin' and tryin' just to do
What I do,

Lovin' Is You!!!

Still Got Love In My Heart

Didn't mean to say it that way
My voice began to rise and tremble
Somehow
And suddenly
What I said before
now I don't mean.
Can't ever make up my mind
                          these days
My heart is pounding
                          faster and faster
My head is hanging down
Streams of salty water
                          roll on my face
My head is throbbing from blows
                          and insults
and my head
and my back
and my legs
and my eyes
Are all sorry you feel this way
I made another mistake
I said something outta line
Maybe I wasn't there on time
Of course
You keep me in check
Everything bad is basically

my fault
in the long run.
Don't know what else to say
'Cept
I'm sorry things turned out this way
Shoulda believed it the first time
Still don't understand
     why I believed
     you loved me
After all those times you
     knocked me upside
     my head
People knew
and they heard me crying and going along with your
 program
But they still smiled at me
when me and the kids
came downstairs
I smiled too
But inside
I felt like a
     PIECE OF SHIT
'Cause I loved you and not me!
     I'm living in shame
Yesterday's dreams have turned into nightmares
Now I must learn to love
     myself again

and leave you behind
Ain't supposed to stay and allow you to hurt me
Repeatedly
I can see clearly now
I will no longer be ashamed
Or afraid to enjoy the life I've been
                              blessed with
It is
What it is
and somewhere along the line
We will always wonder
about one another sometime
Strange
but I still find it
in my heart
to wish you well
I still find that I have
love in my heart
                        and can grow…

Young Mother

Mother
me
wanting you
no matter what
gonna be better
better than me
'cause I had love and good intentions and dreams and
   the burning
desire to do good.
Unfortunately,
it would take way, way more than that
way more…
How was I to know?

Ella Mae

The first time

ever

I

saw your face

I was eleven years old

At first

she was simply, "the pretty lady upstairs" with the
three kids

She came and went with them

went to work and took care of her business

Took care of her dad ---Pop

"the pretty lady upstairs"

 who smiled and laughed when spoken to by some
grown-ups

outside the building talkin'

inside Mommy's apartment partying after she helped
to fix it up

she hung curtains

I watched her make things look real good

Many called and have called her Penny, Miss Penny

She is Mommy, Gee-Ma, Aunt Penny, Auntie

Yet the real, real is ELLA – ELLA MAE though

She didn't stand for no FOOLISHNESS

She meant what she said – "Ju, I'm not playin' with
you!"

She loved and she cared, and she showed up

and she understood life and she was reasonable

Always making sense

Street savvy – Donald said

Flexible

Classy, cool,

Always sexy

Had that Diahann Carroll – Dominique Devereax
   swag going on

Someone you could talk to 'cause she kept it real

Granny's other daughter and Tootsie's other "little
   sister"

Miss Daisy's "best bud"

She let me in her house, her life, her heart

Always treated me good

and put me in my place when necessary

A "Smokey Robinson" girl … and I

"Second That Emotion" --- rocking the "Four Corners"
   dance

An "Aretha Franklin" kind of woman…" Baby, Baby,
   Baby"

Always encouraging

Always there…

Know that I will always remember the ties that bind

Auntie!

Glad I recognize goodness

want you to know

I'm so glad to know you

Appreciate your love and laughter

Gotta tell it like it "tiz"

I love you

immensely

I thank you and Donald thanks you and Angie thanks
  you too

Simply

Loving you!

No Sex In The City

For quite some time, I thought about writing about relationships. I was hesitant because I didn't know how it would be received, in addition to it being a difficult topic. Relationships…High voltage, a gamut of responses would be ignited. The whole idea of two people together, with that in mind one thing led to the other. Together, not together, sometimes together---perpetrating being together. Husbands and wives, boyfriends and girlfriends, the other woman, the jump off. The "he sees me sometimes chick." Wow! It became a bit too much. Having seen myself in one or more of these situations, I had eventually came to a realization and one thing was certain; I brought my best self to the relationship and wanted the best for my partner. Respect, honesty, and love were the primary elements. With those in place, the possibilities for the future were endless. That's what I thought.

I truly believe in love and two people being happy with one another. Shoot, when you feel the goodness and see it reflected in your partner's eyes, you become energized. The force is so powerful that it enhances what you already are, and you are propelled to another level. You do so many wonderful things for yourself, for your mate, and for the world. I know that real love is splendid. Though without respect, all the possibilities for the relationship to thrive become minimized.

Everyone wants to be recognized and know that they have the right to their feelings, beliefs, and principles. No one wants their dream for their life thwarted with disrespect. When one is not regarded or considered in a thoughtful manner, the relationship will not survive. Many of us know that when the relationship is on the downward spiral, onslaughts of not so good feelings emerge, primarily because respect was not valued. Oh boy!

With respect comes honesty. When you respect someone and what they represent, no matter how difficult, the truth must be told. It must be in the forefront of the union; otherwise, someone will be deeply hurt and catapulted into an undesirable condition. A person who is respected should be offered the opportunity to know exactly what kind of relationship they are involved in. Is it a "me for you and you for me" type of thing? Is it a "not on the outside but inside strong" situation? Or is it a "got me going in circles" kind of existence? Most people want to know upfront. They want to be able to make life-changing decisions for themselves. Unfortunately, honesty has not been on the priority list of a great many in their pursuit of happiness.

Love embodies respect and honesty. Love is necessary. Love is wholesome, nurturing and fulfilling. Love is truly beautiful. With all of this at my very core, I have arrived at a "not so comfortable" place for many. They shake their heads and say, "Girl, I don't know how you do it, I gotta have someone."

Or they've said, "You've been celibate for how many years? Girl, Get the cobwebs out, you're crazy!" One of my daughters looked at me with tears in her eyes and said, "Mommy…I don't want to end up like you, with nobody, Oh my God!"

I tried to convey to her that I was fine, better than fine. I wanted her to know that I was in a good place emotionally---not depressed, miserable or lonely. I wanted her to understand that I desired a wholesome, nurturing union. I wanted to be able to be myself, flaws and all. I wanted her to get that I wanted more than some intermittent relationship, filled with stolen moments and hump fests on occasion. It saddened me to hear her say that she didn't want to

"end up like me."

Am I crazy? When I was a little girl, my mother used to call me her "Queen." She held me in high esteem and wanted the very best for me. She wanted me to want the best for myself even if it meant that I had to be alone. I believe that I should truly love myself, and in doing so, I should remove my whole self (mind, body and spirit) out of harm's way. I know what it feels like to be betrayed and violated on a variety of fronts. I know what it feels like to have your health compromised by someone who lacks respect.

Am I crazy? I am a woman willing to love someone with all of my heart and my very best self. In doing so, I expect it to be reciprocated. I am not going to compromise principles when it comes to respect, honesty, and love even if it means I remain alone and celibate. Sure, I would love to hold someone's hand while walking in the park on a warm summer day. I would also enjoy the scent of a man, as I gently stroked his arm while resting my head on his shoulder. I would absolutely cherish the time spent talking on the phone during the wee hours of the morning and spending days enveloped in his loving arms on vacation.

So here I am bringing my honest self, my true self, my sexless self to the forefront. Although initially I was hesitant about writing about relationships and the complexities that ensue, I embraced it from where I am and was able to bring forth some thoughts. Why celibacy? Shoot, I simply want the best for myself and a peace of mind.